To the Esposito family.
with best wishes,
Jeff Chapman-Crane
3/99

RAGSALE

Written by Artie Ann Bates

Illustrated by Jeff Chapman-Crane

Houghton Mifflin Company
Boston 1995

Library of Congress Cataloging-in-Publication Data

Bates, Artie Ann.
    Ragsale / Artie Ann Bates ; illustrated by Jeff Chapman-Crane.
        p.   cm.
    Summary: Jessann and her family spend Saturday going to the
ragsales of their Appalachian town.
    ISBN 0-395-70030-2
    [1. Shopping—Fiction.   2. Appalachian Region—Fiction.]
I. Chapman-Crane, Jeff, ill.   II. Title.
PZ7.B29445Rag   1995   94-17366
[E]—dc20   CIP
                              AC

Printed in the United States of America

HOR   10   9   8   7   6   5   4   3   2   1

The wind stings my face as I wrap a scarf around my head. Mommy is warming up the car, with a cloud of fumes around it. As I climb into the back seat with my sister Eunice, Daddy hollers from the front porch, "You all don't forget to come home."

Mommy yells back, with a sassy smile, "Well, sometime this evenin', when we get through ragsaling."

We are up early this Saturday going to the ragsales. Mamaw, Aunt Mary Jane, and cousin Billie Jo are waiting for us at Elk Creek. We'll stop at one sale right after another. Today we are going to the sale at Stuart Robinson School, Montgomery Creek, and Hindman. I'm hoping to find a pair of red mittens for riding the sled.

The Stuart Robinson ragsale is at Mommy's old high school, so she always sees people she knows. It's the first of the month and shipments of clothes come in from up north. The wooden floors creak as the women pour in. Sometimes the men come too, but they stand outside and whittle, their breath making fog as they laugh.

We take secondhand clothes off the tables, trying them on over our own in the aisle. Some ragsales have a dressing room, some just a mirror. We will feel dusty when we get home this evening, and change clothes, and wash our hands. Used clothes always smell like an empty box, or one with moth balls.

Aunt Mary Jane whistles Old Regular Baptist songs as she looks. I play peep-eye with the baby holding onto her mommy's dresstail.

Blouses and sweaters are twenty-five cents. Shoes are a dollar or, if they have broken-down heels, maybe a dime. Mommy gets all her dresses at the ragsale. I never did see her buy one from a store, and she is a schoolteacher. She says, "Why pay a lot for clothes when I can fix these up from the ragsale?" Now and then she finds one with the store tags still on it.

Women carefully lift workclothes from the big-mouthed barrels and wooden tables, holding shirts, longjohns, and bib overalls up against the light to check for holes or stains. They want sturdy cotton things for their husbands to wear in the mines and cornfields, to keep them warm in winter and soak up sweat in summer. They find plenty of school clothes for the children.

Digging to the bottoms of cardboard barrels, metal rims catch under our bellies. The barrels cough out their broken-in negligees and corsets, lace strings dangling. Eunice and I try these on under our dresses, like the older ladies, but they won't stay up. We don't have enough belly.

This ragsale has a whole table of women's stuff. A pearl necklace matches the hanging earrings Eunice got. That silver pin will go good in the red hat with a veil, and these stockings with a line up the back look like Elizabeth Taylor. Now all we need are some patent leather high heels. We know about the used red lipstick. Mamaw says, "Don't touch it, Jessann, you never know who might have used it!"

Handed-down dishes, like pitchers and gravy bowls, are fifteen cents. Mamaw serves her gravy, with grease floating on top, in bowls like these. She is an old-time cook. Ceramic dogs to use as doorstops are two dollars. Some people put them in their front yards. They do look bright after the yard is swept clean.

Billie Jo stays longest in the books, shelving through paperbacks with torn edges. We find *National Geographic* and look at pictures of young'uns in bright clothes from islands we can't pronounce. Once we found one about our mountains. It showed a woman crossing the creek on a log footbridge, carrying a basket.

We stand in line to check out. Mommy has two armloads of stuff. "That will be $3.75," the lady says. She figured it on a paper bag. Mamaw gets a few dresses, an apron, and a flour board. Aunt Mary Jane has a pair of shoes and Billie Jo some westerns.

At Montgomery Creek we look at furniture. Aunt Mary Jane finds an end table with claw feet over shiny glass marbles. Mamaw gets a basket for her *Life* magazines, to set by the fireplace. Mommy buys a faded picture that might be by a famous artist because it says *Winslow H.* in the corner. Billie Jo picks out a book of poems by Emily Dickinson.

The Hindman ragsale is in an old store building. It has glass windows in front with GROCERY AND FEED printed in yellow paint. The clothes are mostly hanging on racks, which makes looking easier. I wonder what sailor wore this navy jacket with anchor buttons. Mommy finds some blouses in my size and pants for my little brother, William.

We carry our treasures to the car, tired legs and thinking of supper. As Mommy opens the trunk I run back for a bundle. They have surprise clothes in them and cost fifty cents. "Don't open it until we get home," I know Mommy will say. I feel the bundle to see if I can guess. Eunice gets one, too. Maybe it will have the mittens I want.

Daddy sees us coming up the yard and steps onto the porch. He leans against the banister and spits tobacco juice off into the grass. He smiles as if he knows something we don't. "Did you have a good sale?"

Pulling up the steps with bags in her arms, Mommy replies, "Always do." My scarf flies in the wind as Eunice and I tear open our bundles.

About the Author

Artie Ann Bates grew up in the Appalachian area of eastern Kentucky of which she writes. Ragsales were an important part of her childhood and Artie Ann wrote this story to help preserve her Appalachian culture and heritage for children today. "Ragsales are a special kind of used clothing store, and when I was a little girl we went to the ragsale about every weekend. Wearing used clothes is a way of not wasting things that are still good. While there used to be a lot of ragsales in eastern Kentucky, there aren't as many now, but going to them is as much fun as ever."

About the Illustrator

Jeff Chapman-Crane is a freelance artist who lives and works in the mountains of eastern Kentucky. His work reflects his experiences growing up in Appalachia. He is especially concerned with presenting a more authentic and compassionate portrayal of Appalachian life than the stereotypical images so often associated with the region. Jeff Chapman-Crane, together with his artist wife, Sharman, and their son, Evan, operates Valley of the Winds Art Gallery in Eolia, Kentucky, where the family create and display their work.